This book belongs to

LADYBIRD BOOKS

UK | USA | Canada | Ireland | Australia
India | New Zealand | South Africa

Ladybird Books is part of the Penguin Random House group of companies whose addresses
can be found at global.penguinrandomhouse.com.
ladybird.com

Penguin
Random House
UK

First published 2015
001

Copyright © Coolabi Productions Limited, Smallfilms Limited and Peter Firmin, 2015
Written by Daniel Postgate
Illustrations by Irina Golina

Ladybird and the Ladybird logo are registered or unregistered trademarks owned by Ladybird Books Ltd

The moral right of the author, illustrator and copyright holders has been asserted

Printed in China

A CIP catalogue record for this book is available from the British Library

ISBN: 978–0–241–19598–7

THE BRILLIANT
SURPRISE

DANIEL POSTGATE

Granny

Major

Mother

Iron Chicken

Froglets

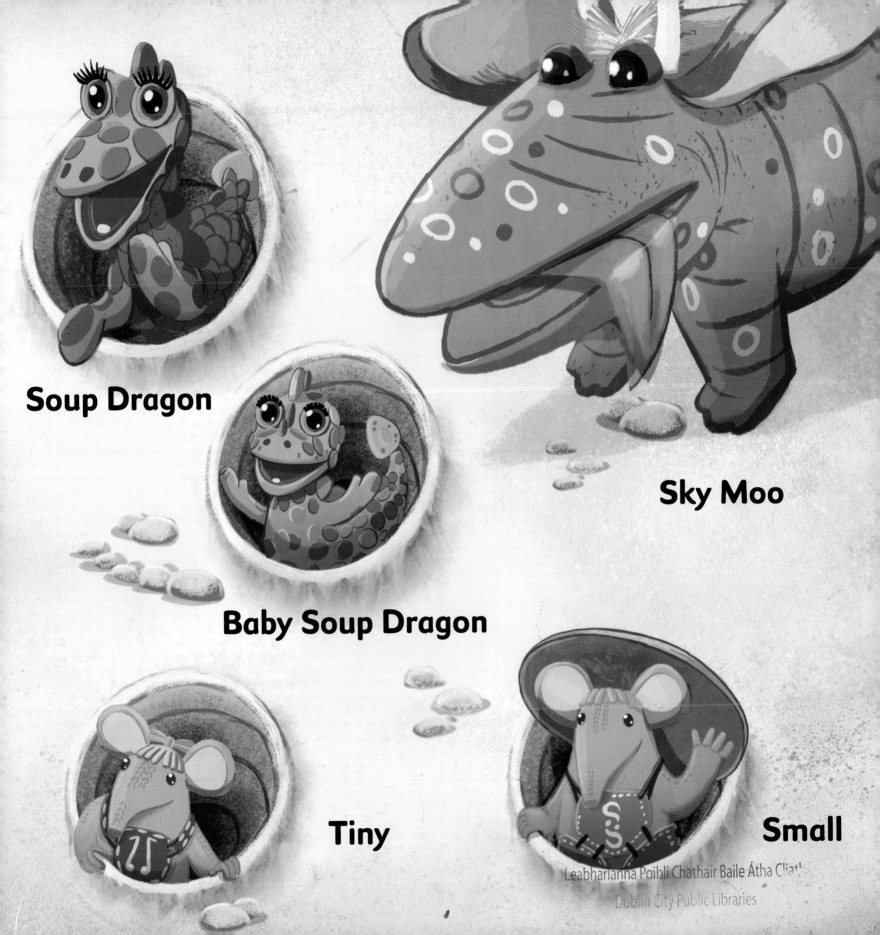

Soup Dragon

Baby Soup Dragon

Sky Moo

Tiny

Small

The Iron Chicken sat on her metal nest, busily looking for interesting things in space.

Suddenly she saw something interesting – very interesting indeed!

Bleep, bleep, bleep!

Deep inside the Clangers' planet, Tiny Clanger
got a message on her special radio hat.

"It's coming!"

the Iron Chicken clucked

with excitement.

"What's coming?" asked Tiny.

"Tell Small! He'll know!"
squawked the chicken.

Tiny told her brother, Small: "The Iron Chicken says, 'It's coming!'"

Small hopped . . .

. . . and skipped and jigged about.

"Hurray!" he sang.
"We must tell Mother!"

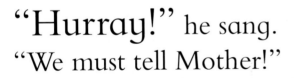

"It's coming!"
yelled Small.

"Oh, how wonderful!"
cried Mother. "Granny, wake up!
We must decorate the Music Trees
with flowers."

Small ran through the caves.
"It's coming! It's coming!"
he called as he ran.

The Glow-Buzzers bobbed and buzzed around him.

They were very pleased to hear such news . . .

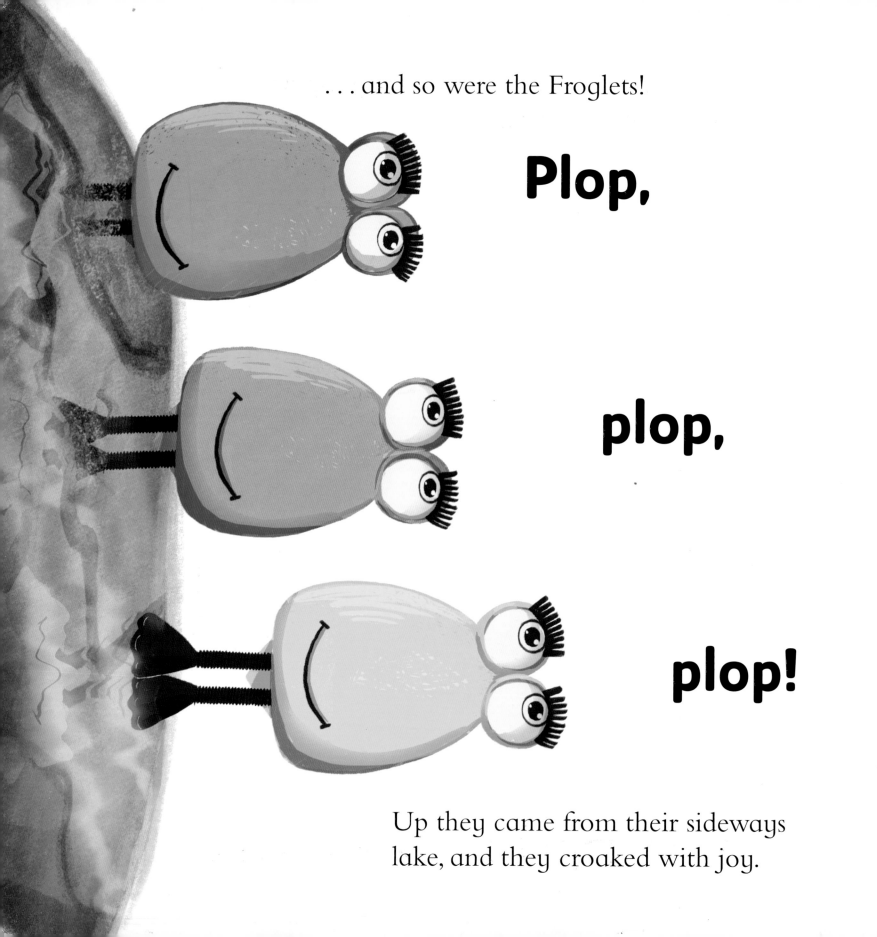

. . . and so were the Froglets!

Plop,

plop,

plop!

Up they came from their sideways lake, and they croaked with joy.

Poor Tiny. She didn't know what was going on.
And Small wouldn't tell her.

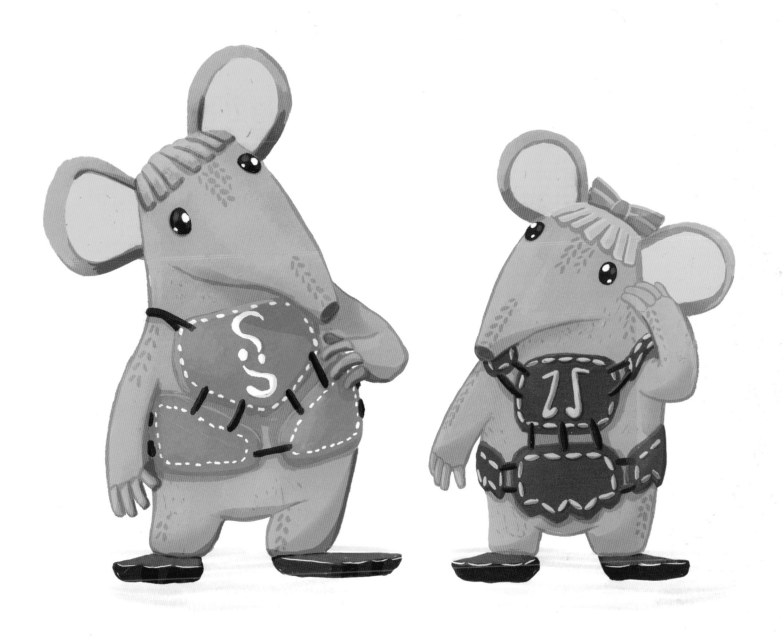

"It's a surprise," was all he would say.

Small hurried off to tell the Soup Dragon and her baby.

"Wondlerful newslly!"
burbled the Soup Dragon. "I shall makle
some lovellly bubbly soupley doupley."

And she went down into her well to
make her very best soup in celebration.

Major Clanger was busy inventing
in his workshop when Small rushed in
to tell him the news.

Of course, Major was delighted.
"We must tell everyone, absolutely everyone!" he exclaimed.

"But – but – but –"
said Tiny, quite baffled
by it all.

"No time for buts!" Major laughed.
"Just help me with my rocket."

Heave, heave, heave!

Major, Small and Tiny
pulled the rocket out
through the big brass doors.

"Three, two, one!" counted Major.
Off went his rocket, high into the sky . . .

Whoosh! went the rocket.

Bang! went the rocket.

And it filled the sky with brilliant little stars, which flashed and fizzled and popped, just like a firework.

Major's firework-rocket worked a treat.

The Hoot Planet, with all the Hoots playing their lovely music, came drifting down to the Clangers' planet.

The Sky Moos came too, flapping their great big ears and mooing joyfully.

Soon everyone had gathered together – Clangers,
Froglets, Glow-Buzzers, Hoots, Soup Dragons,
Sky Moos and the Iron Chicken.

"It's coming! It's coming!"

they all sang, hooted, mooed, croaked, clucked and buzzed.

"But what? What is coming?" wondered Tiny.
Then she saw . . .

It was a comet. A great big fantastic comet with a tail of bright, tiny stars that lit up the sky with every colour of the rainbow. It came roaring over the Clangers' little blue planet.

"Ooooo

Oooooo!"

everyone exclaimed at the marvellous sight.

The Clangers raised their soupy
tankards to greet their beautiful visitor.

"Quick, you must make a wish!" Mother told Tiny. "Last time it came, Small made a wish, and now it is your turn."
"What did Small wish for?" asked Tiny.

"He wished for a lovely little sister,"
said Mother, "and his wish came true."
"It was me!" whispered Tiny.
"Yes, my lovely child," said Mother.

Tiny closed her eyes tight and tried her hardest
to think of something new to wish for.

Then she opened her eyes and said, "I can't think of anything."
She ran and hugged her brother, Small. "Everything is perfect,
just the way it is."

The End